THE GREAT SOAP-BUBBLE RIDE

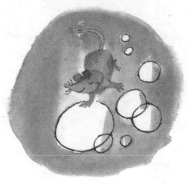

Mimi Mouse lived in an old stone farmhouse with Fontina, her mother, and Herbert, her father.

Hundreds of aunts, uncles, and cousins lived in their neighborhood. But Mimi was lucky. She lived in the cellar of the very best house of all.

It was a beautiful house. Her
great-grandpa had discovered it.
Mimi was born in it. The whole
family came to her house for
holidays. Everyone knew it was
a special family place. But Mimi,
Herbert, and Fontina knew best
of all.

Herbert Mouse was a great
storyteller. His favorite stories
were about the Mouse family
and their home.

"Yes, Grandpa found this house
by mistake," Herbert would say.
His neat, little mustache quivered
as he talked.

"Not this story again," everyone would groan. But they would stay. They would listen again and again.

Herbert went on.
"Old Farmer Fields was
collecting stones to build the
walls of this house," he said.
"And Grandpa tripped over the
biggest rock pile. Got a big
bump on his head, too. Grandpa
thought he'd rest a while. By the
time he felt better, the house was
finished. So he decided to stay."
As always, Herbert laughed
when he finished the story.

Life was nice in the cozy, dark cellar. The farmer's lazy cat didn't go farther than the barn. No one remembered to set new mousetraps.

And the old stone walls kept out
cold winds and wet storms.
Nothing much happened until
Georgia Fields turned eight years
old.

Mimi Mouse knew all six of the children who lived upstairs. At least she knew them from their knees down. What Mimi *didn't* know was what happened when Georgia Fields turned eight—it became Georgia's job to wash her family's clothes.

14

The washing machine was in the cellar (not far from the water heater where Mimi slept). Clotheslines crisscrossed the room. For years, Mr. and Mrs. Fields carried down clothes baskets every Saturday morning.

Together, they emptied the baskets. The light clothes went into one pile. The dark things went into another. They talked about their work. They talked about their children. They talked about their farm. They were so busy. They never noticed the mice.

But Georgia was different. She
wasn't interested in the wash.
So she noticed everything else.
The very first morning Georgia
Fields did the wash, she
discovered Mimi.

The door to the cellar opened in
the dark. The light went on.
"Eek, a mouse!" screamed
Georgia.

Mimi had been doing her
morning sit-ups. She hid under
the bottom step when she heard
Georgia.

"Eek, a girl!" screamed Mimi.

The clothes basket tumbled
down. Light and dark clothes
streamed into the cellar. They
landed right on top of Mimi.

20

Georgia was so surprised that she tumbled down, too. She landed right on top of the clothes. Mimi was at the very bottom of the pile.

"You're squashing me!" she
squeaked.
Georgia looked surprised to hear
a mouse talk so clearly.

"Why are you in my house?
Shoo! Shoo! Go away," Georgia
said.
"*Your* house?" asked Mimi. "This
is *our* house."

"Do you mean there are more mice?" asked Georgia.
"Yes, of course," said Mimi.
"My mother and father live here, too."

"Three mice?" shouted Georgia.
"You'll all have to move out.
Right away!"
"That's silly," said Mimi. "This is
our home. We've lived here for
years. Ever since your grandpa
built the place. Maybe *you*
should move out."

Georgia and Mimi were getting
very excited. Herbert and
Fontina came out to see what
was happening.

"No one is moving out," said
Fontina calmly. "We have
always shared this house. And
we always will. You two might
as well be friends."

Mimi and Georgia looked at
each other. They both had gentle
faces.

28

"Will you help me pick up all
the clothes?" asked Georgia.
"We'll all help," offered Fontina.
The three mice scampered
around. Soon all the clothes were
back in the basket.

Georgia carried the basket to the washing machine. Then Mimi pulled out all the light clothes. She was especially good at finding socks. And with six children, there were a lot of socks!

Herbert pulled out the dark clothes. Fontina made neat piles. Georgia poured one cup of soap into the machine and turned it on. Water sprayed into the machine.

"This reminds me of a great
story," said Herbert.
Herbert told about the time his
Uncle Morris crawled into the
washing machine.

"He couldn't get out," laughed Herbert. "He stayed in for nine washes. Uncle Morris was the world's cleanest mouse. Of course, he always seemed a little dizzy after that."

Herbert told Georgia and Mimi
many stories. Together, they
listened. They laughed. They
hung socks to dry on the lines.
They folded clean, sweet-
smelling clothes. Georgia seemed
happy with the Mouse family.
But when the wash was all done,
she frowned.

"Fun is fun," said Georgia. "But
you'll have to go. We can't have
mice running high and low."

Then she picked up the wash and climbed the stairs. The light went out. The door closed. It was dark again.

Many Saturdays went by. Each washday Mimi and her family helped. Each time Herbert told them funny stories. Mimi and Georgia laughed together. But at the end Georgia always frowned.

And she said, "Fun is fun. But you'll have to go. We can't have mice running high and low."

Then one Saturday everything
changed.

That day Herbert told one of his best stories. Georgia listened hard. She paid no attention to her work. She didn't stop after putting one cup of soap into the washing machine. She kept pouring. Soon ten cups of soap swirled around in the washing machine. And no one noticed.

As the four friends talked,
bubbles floated out of the
machine. At first they came
slowly. Then great bursts of
bubbles streamed out.

Soon they covered the washing
machine. Bubbles crept over the
floor. Bubbles tumbled over the
first three stairs. Bubbles piled
higher and higher. And no one
noticed.

42

Then a great wave of bubbles
rushed out of the machine. It
swept the mice right off their
toes. They kicked. They swam.
They rode the giant wave of
bubbles. But it was just too
much for them. And they began
to sink.

Georgia watched the mice being
washed away. She tried to reach
them. But new waves of bubbles
got in her way. She scooped
great puffs of bubbles away.

Finally, Georgia spotted Herbert
and Fontina. She lifted them out
of the bubbles. She put them up
on the clothesline to dry off.
Then she went back for Mimi.

She searched. She worked. She
worried. And finally, she found
Mimi. The little mouse was
almost lost. But Georgia rescued
her. And they both felt great
about that!

From then on they met often.
But now Georgia did not frown.
Instead she smiled. And she said,
"I've learned from you, my
friends so small, that there is
room for one and all."

The mice never forgot how
Georgia Fields saved them.
And Herbert Mouse had
a new favorite story.
From then on, he told
everyone all about the
Great Soap-Bubble Ride.